CALYPSO
Cousteau

LITTLE SIMON
Simon & Schuster Building, Rockefeller Center
1230 Avenue of the Americas, New York, New York 10020
Copyright © 1991 by Hachette, France, and The Cousteau Society, Inc. English Translation
copyright © 1992 by The Cousteau Society, Inc. All rights reserved including the right of
reproduction in whole or in part in any form. Originally published in France by Hachette
Jeunesse as *PINGUINS*. LITTLE SIMON and colophon are trademarks of Simon & Schuster.
Manufactured in Singapore   10 9 8 7 6 5 4 3 2

Library of Congress Cataloging-in-Publication Data
Penguins / the Cousteau Society.   p.   cm.   Summary: An introduction to the penguin,
the unusual bird that cannot fly because its wings are too small.   1. Penguins — Juvenile
literature.   [1. Penguins.]   I. Cousteau Society.   QL696.S473P45   1992
598.4'41 — dc20   91-35229   CIP
ISBN: 0-671-77058-6

The Cousteau Society

PENGUINS

LITTLE SIMON

Published by Simon & Schuster
New York   London   Toronto   Sydney   Tokyo   Singapore

THE GENTOO PENGUIN

Bird

Adult weight and size
13 pounds, 2½ feet

Life span
10-15 years

Food
Krill, squid, small fish

Reproduction
Mates once a year. Two eggs are laid and
alternately incubated by the male and the female.

Lives in the Antarctic region.

Populations relatively stable.

These are penguins, with their warm,
thick coats of black and white feathers.

The mother penguin lays two big eggs. Both mother

and father take turns keeping the chicks safe and warm.

Mother searches for food for the chicks, swimming

and leaping through icy water.

She keeps an eye on the shore.

Then finally, the feast begins!

The young penguins grow up together,

surrounded and protected by their parents.

Penguins are most unusual birds.

They can't fly because their wings are too small.

They use their flipper-like wings

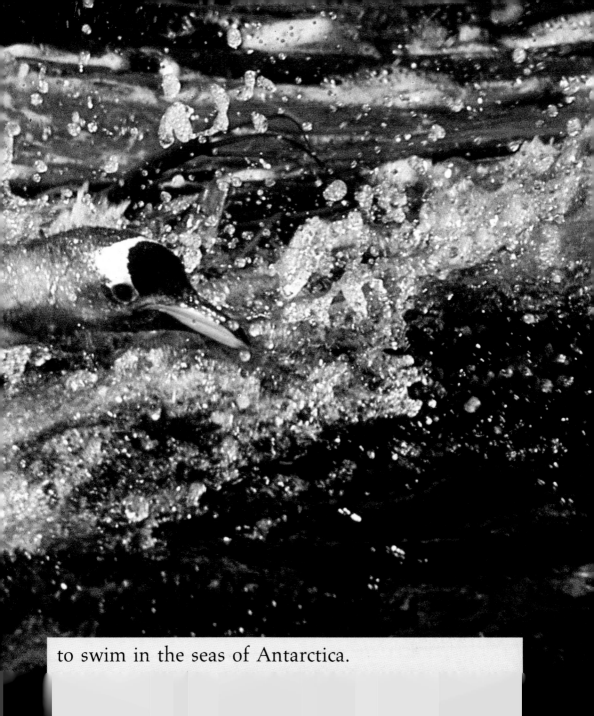

to swim in the seas of Antarctica.